PAUL BOWLES

THINGS GONE AND THINGS STILL HERE

BLACK SPARROW PRESS : SANTA BARBARA : 1977

THINGS GONE AND THINGS STILL HERE.
Copyright © 1977 by Paul Bowles.

All rights reserved. Printed in the United States of America. No part of this book may be used or reproduced in any manner whatsoever without written permission except in the case of brief quotations embodied in critical articles and reviews. For information address Black Sparrow Press, P.O. Box 3993, Santa Barbara, CA 93105.

ACKNOWLEDGEMENT

The author would like to thank the editors of *Antaeus, Bastard Angel, Prose* and *Rolling Stone* where several of these stories previously appeared.

LIBRARY OF CONGRESS CATALOGING IN PUBLICATION DATA

Bowles, Paul Frederic, 1911-
   Things gone and things still here.

   CONTENTS: Allal.—Mejdoub.—You have left your lotus pods on the bus.—The Fqih. [etc.]
   I. Title.
PZ3.B6826Tg   [PS3552.O874]   813'.5'4   77-8030
ISBN 0-87685-341-6 (trade paper edition)
ISBN 0-87685-342-4 (trade cloth edition)
ISBN 0-87685-343-2 (signed cloth edition)

by Paul Bowles

Novels

The Sheltering Sky (1949)
Let It Come Down (1952)
The Spider's House (1955)
Up Above the World (1966)

Collections of Stories

The Delicate Prey (1950)
A Hundred Camels in the Courtyard (1962)
The Time of Friendship (1967)
Things Gone & Things Still Here (1977)

Travel Essays

Yallah (Photographs by Peter W. Haeberlin) (1957)
Their Heads Are Green and Their Hands Are Blue (1963)

Poetry

Two Poems (1933)
Scenes (1968)
The Thicket of Spring (1972)
Next to Nothing (1977)

Texts Taped and Translated from the Moghrebi

A Life Full Of Holes (Driss ben Hamed Charhadi) (1964)
Love With A Few Hairs (Mohammed Mrabet) (1968)
The Lemon (Mohammed Mrabet) (1968)
M'Hashish (Mohammed Mrabet) (1970)
The Boy Who Set the Fire (Mohammed Mrabet) (1974)
Look & Move On (Mohammed Mrabet) (1976)
Harmless Poisons, Blameless Sins (Mohammed Mrabet) (1976)

Autobiography

Without Stopping (1972)

TABLE OF CONTENTS

Allal	7
Mejdoub	23
You Have Left Your Lotus Pods on the Bus	31
The Fqih	43
Istikhara, Anaya, Medagan and the Medaganat	49
The Waters of Izli	55
Afternoon With Antaeus	61
Reminders of Bouselham	69
Things Gone and Things Still Here	83

Allal

He was born in the hotel where his mother worked. The hotel had only three dark rooms which gave on a courtyard behind the bar. Beyond was another smaller patio with many doors. This was where the servants lived, and where Allal spent his childhood.

The Greek who owned the hotel had sent Allal's mother away. He was indignant because she, a girl of fourteen, had dared to give birth while she was working for him. She would not say who the father was, and it angered him to reflect that he himself had not taken advantage of the situation while he had had the chance. He gave the girl three months' wages and told her to go home to Marrakech. Since the cook and his wife liked the girl and offered to let her live with them for a while, he agreed that she might stay on until the baby was big enough to travel. She remained in the back patio for a few months with the cook and his wife, and then one day she disappeared, leaving the baby behind. No one heard of her again.

As soon as Allal was old enough to carry things, they set him to work. It was not long before he could fetch a pail of water from the well behind the hotel. The cook and his wife were childless, so that he played alone.

When he was somewhat older he began to wander over the empty table-land outside. There was nothing else up here but the barracks, and they were enclosed by a high blind wall of red adobe. Everything else was below in the valley: the town, the gardens, and the river winding southward among the thousands of palm trees. He could sit on a point of rock far above and look down at the people walking in the alleys of the town. It was only later that he visited the place and saw what the inhabitants were like. Because he had been left behind by his mother they called him a son of sin, and laughed when they looked at him. It seemed to him that in this way they hoped to make him into a shadow, in order not to have to think of him as real and alive. He awaited with dread the time when he would have to go each morning to the town and work. For the moment he helped in the kitchen and served the officers from the barracks, along with the few motorists who passed through the region. He got small tips in the restaurant, and free food and lodging in a cell of the servants' quarters, but the Greek gave him no wages. Eventually he reached an age when this situation seemed shameful, and he went of his own accord to the town below and began to work, along with other boys of his age, helping to make the mud bricks people used for building their houses.

Living in the town was much as he had imagined it would be. For two years he stayed in a room behind a blacksmith's shop, leading a life without quarrels, and saving whatever money he did not have to spend to keep himself alive. Far from making any friends during this time, he formed a thorough hatred for the people of the town, who never allowed him to forget that he was a son of sin, and therefore not like others, but *meskhot*—damned. Then he found a small house, not much more than a hut, in the palm groves outside the town. The rent was low and no one lived nearby. He went to live there, where the only sound was the wind in the trees, and avoided the people of the town when he could.

One hot summer evening shortly after sunset he was walking under the arcades that faced the town's main square. A few paces ahead of him an old man in a white turban was trying to shift a heavy sack from one shoulder to the other. Suddenly it fell to the ground, and Allal stared as two long dark forms flowed out of it and disappeared into the shadows. The old man pounced upon the sack and fastened the top of it, at the same time beginning to shout: Look out for the snakes! Help me find my snakes!

Many people turned quickly around and walked back the way they had come. Others stood at some distance, watching. A few called to the old man: Find your snakes fast and get them out of here! Why are they here? We don't want snakes in this town!

Hopping up and down in his anxiety, the old man turned to Allal. Watch this for me a minute, my son. He pointed at the sack lying on the earth at his feet, and snatching up a basket he had been carrying, went swiftly around the corner into an alley. Allal stood where he was. No one passed by.

It was not long before the old man returned, panting with triumph. When the onlookers in the square saw him again, they began to call out, this time to Allal: Show that berrani the way out of the town! He has no right to carry those things in here. Out! Out!

Allal picked up the big sack and said to the old man: Come on.

They left the square and went through the alleys until they were at the edge of town. The old man looked up then, saw the palm trees black against the fading sky ahead, and turned to the boy beside him.

Come on, said Allal again, and he went to the left along the rough path that led to his house. The old man stood perplexed.

You can stay with me tonight, Allal told him.

And these? he said, pointing first at the sack and then at the basket. They have to be with me.

Allal grinned. They can come.

When they were sitting in the house Allal looked at the sack and the basket. I'm not like the rest of them here, he said.

It made him feel good to hear the words being spoken. He made a contemptuous gesture. Afraid to walk through the square because of a snake. You saw them.

The old man scratched his chin. Snakes are like people, he said. You have to get to know them. Then you can be their friends.

Allal hesitated before he asked: Do you ever let them out?

Always, the old man said with energy. It's bad for them to be inside like this. They've got to be healthy when they get to Taroudant, or the man there won't buy them.

He began a long story about his life as a hunter

of snakes, explaining that each year he made a voyage to Taroudant to see a man who bought them for the Aissaoua snake-charmers in Marrakech. Allal made tea while he listened, and brought out a bowl of kif paste to eat with the tea. Later, when they were sitting comfortably in the midst of the pipe-smoke, the old man chuckled. Allal turned to look at him.

Shall I let them out?

Fine!

But you must sit still and keep quiet. Move the lamp nearer.

He untied the sack, shook it a bit, and returned to where he had been sitting. Then in silence Allal watched the long bodies move cautiously out into the light. Among the cobras were others with markings so delicate and perfect that they seemed to have been designed and painted by an artist. One reddish-gold serpent, which coiled itself lazily in the middle of the floor, he found particularly beautiful. As he stared at it, he felt a great desire to own it and have it always with him.

The old man was talking. I've spent my whole life with snakes, he said. I could tell you some things about them. Did you know that if you give them majoun you can make them do what you want, and without saying a word? I swear by Allah!

Allal's face assumed a doubtful air. He did not question the truth of the other's statement, but rather the likelihood of his being able to put the knowledge to use. For it was at that moment that the idea of actually taking the snake first came into his head. He was thinking that whatever he was to do must be done quickly, for the old man would be leaving in the morning. Suddenly he felt a great impatience.

Put them away so I can cook dinner, he whispered. Then he sat admiring the ease with which the old man picked up each one by its head and slipped it into the sack. Once again he dropped two of the snakes into the basket, and one of these, Allal noted, was the red one. He imagined he could see the shining of its scales through the lid of the basket.

As he set to work preparing the meal Allal tried to think of other things. Then, since the snake remained in his mind in spite of everything, he began to devise a way of getting it. While he squatted over the fire in a corner, he mixed some kif paste in a bowl of milk and set it aside.

The old man continued to talk. That was good luck, getting the two snakes back like that, in the middle of the town. You can never be sure what people are going to do when they find out you're carrying snakes. Once in El Kelaa they took all of them and killed them, one after the other, in front of me. A year's work. I had to go back home and start all over again.

Even as they ate, Allal saw that his guest was growing sleepy. How will things happen? he wondered. There was no way of knowing beforehand precisely what he was going to do, and the prospect of having to handle the snake worried him. It could kill me, he thought.

Once they had eaten, drunk tea and smoked a few pipes of kif, the old man lay back on the floor and said he was going to sleep. Allal sprang up. In here! he told him, and led him to his own mat in an alcove. The old man lay down and swiftly fell asleep.

Several times during the next half hour Allal

went to the alcove and peered in, but neither the body in its burnous nor the head in its turban had stirred.

First he got out his blanket, and after tying three of its corners together, spread it on the floor with the fourth corner facing the basket. Then he set the bowl of milk and kif paste on the blanket. As he loosened the strap from the cover of the basket the old man coughed. Allal stood immobile, waiting to hear the cracked voice speak. A small breeze had sprung up, making the palm branches rasp one against the other, but there was no further sound from the alcove. He crept to the far side of the room and squatted by the wall, his gaze fixed on the basket.

Several times he thought he saw the cover move slightly, but each time he decided he had been mistaken. Then he caught his breath. The shadow along the base of the basket was moving. One of the creatures had crept out from the far side. It waited for a while before continuing into the light, but when it did, Allal breathed a prayer of thanks. It was the red and gold one.

When finally it decided to go to the bowl, it made a complete tour around the edge, looking in from all sides, before lowering its head toward the milk. Allal watched, fearful that the foreign flavor of the kif paste might repel it. The snake remained there without moving.

He waited a half hour or more. The snake stayed where it was, its head in the bowl. From time to time Allal glanced at the basket, to be certain that the second snake was still in it. The breeze went on, rubbing the palm branches together. When he decided it was time, he rose slowly, and keeping an eye on the basket where apparently the other snake still slept, he reached over and gathered together the three tied corners of the blanket. Then he lifted the fourth corner, so that both the snake and the bowl slid to the bottom of the improvised sack. The snake moved slightly, but he did not think it was angry. He knew exactly where he would hide it: between some rocks in the dry river bed.

Holding the blanket in front of him he opened the door and stepped out under the stars. It was not far up the road, to a group of high palms, and then to the left down into the oued. There was a space between the boulders where the bundle would be invisible. He pushed it in with care, and hurried back to the house. The old man was asleep.

There was no way of being sure that the other snake was still in the basket, so Allal picked up his burnous and went outside. He shut the door and lay down on the ground to sleep.

Before the sun was in the sky the old man was awake, lying in the alcove coughing. Allal jumped up, went inside, and began to make a fire in the mijmah. A minute later he heard the other exclaim: They're loose again! Out of the basket! Stay where you are and I'll find them.

It was not long before the old man grunted with satisfaction. I have the black one! he cried. Allal did not look up from the corner where he crouched, and the old man came over, waving a cobra. Now I've got to find the other one.

He put the snake away and continued to search. When the fire was blazing, Allal turned and said: Do you want me to help you look for it?

No, no! Stay where you are.

Allal boiled the water and made the tea, and still

the old man was crawling on his knees, lifting boxes and pushing sacks. His turban had slipped off and his face ran with sweat.

Come and have tea, Allal told him.

The old man did not seem to have heard him at first. Then he rose and went into the alcove, where he rewound his turban. When he came out he sat down with Allal, and they had breakfast.

Snakes are very clever, the old man said. They can get into places that don't exist. I've moved everything in this house.

After they had finished eating, they went outside and looked for the snake between the close-growing trunks of the palms near the house. When the old man was convinced that it was gone, he went sadly back in.

That was a good snake, he said at last. And now I'm going to Taroudant.

They said good-bye, and the old man took his sack and basket and started up the road toward the highway.

All day long as he worked, Allal thought of the snake, but it was not until sunset that he was able to go to the rocks in the oued and pull out the blanket. He carried it back to the house in a high state of excitement.

Before he untied the blanket, he filled a wide dish with milk and kif paste, and set it on the floor. He ate three spoonfuls of the paste himself and sat back to watch, drumming on the low wooden teatable with his fingers. Everything happened just as he had hoped. The snake came slowly out of the blanket, and very soon had found the dish and was drinking the milk. As long as it drank he kept drumming; when it had finished and raised its head to look at him, he stopped, and it crawled back inside the blanket.

Later that evening he put down more milk, and drummed again on the table. After a time the snake's head appeared, and finally all of it, and the entire pattern of action was repeated.

That night and every night thereafter, Allal sat with the snake, while with infinite patience he sought to make it his friend. He never attempted to touch it, but soon he was able to summon it, keep it in front of him for as long as he pleased, merely by tapping on the table, and dismiss it at will. For the first week or so he used the kif paste; then he tried the routine without it. In the end the results were the same. After that he fed it only milk and eggs.

Then one evening as his friend lay gracefully coiled in front of him, he began to think of the old man, and formed an idea that put all other things out of his mind. There had not been any kif paste in the house for several weeks, and he decided to make some. He bought the ingredients the following day, and after work he prepared the paste. When it was done, he mixed a large amount of it in a bowl with milk and set it down for the snake. Then he himself ate four spoonfuls, washing them down with tea.

He quickly undressed, and moving the table so that he could reach it, stretched out naked on a mat near the door. This time he continued to tap on the table, even after the snake had finished drinking the milk. It lay still, observing him, as if it were in doubt that the familiar drumming came from the brown body in front of it.

Seeing that even after a long time it remained

where it was, staring at him with its stony yellow eyes, Allal began to say to it over and over: Come here. He knew it could not hear his voice, but he believed it could feel his mind as he urged it. You can make them do what you want, without saying a word, the old man had told him.

Although the snake did not move, he went on repeating his command, for by now he knew it was going to come. And after another long wait, all at once it lowered its head and began to move toward him. It reached his hip and slid along his leg. Then it climbed up his leg and lay for a time across his chest. Its body was heavy and tepid, its scales wonderfully smooth. After a time it came to rest, coiled in the space between his head and his shoulder.

By this time the kif paste had completely taken over Allal's mind. He lay in a state of pure delight, feeling the snake's head against his own, without a thought save that he and the snake were together. The patterns forming and melting behind his eyelids seemed to be the same ones that covered the snake's back. Now and then in a huge frenzied movement they all swirled up and shattered into fragments which swiftly became one great yellow eye, split through the middle by the narrow vertical pupil that pulsed with his own heartbeat. Then the eye would recede, through shifting shadow and sunlight, until only the designs of the scales were left, swarming with renewed insistence as they merged and separated. At last the eye returned, so huge this time that it had no edge around it, its pupil dilated to form an aperture almost wide enough for him to enter. As he stared at the blackness within, he understood that he was being slowly propelled toward the opening. He put out his hands to touch the polished surface of the eye on each side, and as he did this he felt the pull from within. He slid through the crack and was swallowed by darkness.

On awakening Allal felt that he had returned from somewhere far away. He opened his eyes and saw, very close to him, what looked like the flank of an enormous beast, covered with coarse stiff hair. There was a repeated vibration in the air, like distant thunder curling around the edges of the sky. He sighed, or imagined that he did, for his breath made no sound. Then he shifted his head a bit, to try and see beyond the mass of hairs beside him. Next he saw the ear, and he knew he was looking at his own head from the outside. He had not expected this; he had hoped only that his friend would come in and share his mind with him. But it did not strike him as being at all strange; he merely said to himself that now he was seeing through the eyes of the snake, rather than through his own.

Now he understood why the serpent had been so wary of him: from here the boy was a monstrous creature, with all the bristles on his head and his breathing that vibrated inside him like a far-off storm.

He uncoiled himself and glided across the floor to the alcove. There was a break in the mud wall wide enough to let him out. When he had pushed himself through, he lay full length on the ground in the crystalline moonlight, staring at the strangeness of the landscape, where shadows were not shadows.

He crawled around the side of the house and started up the road toward the town, rejoicing in a sense of freedom different from any he had ever imagined. There was no feeling of having a body, for he was perfectly contained in the skin that covered him. It was beautiful to caress the earth with the length of his belly as he moved along the silent road, smelling the sharp veins of wormwood in the wind. When the voice of the muezzin floated out over the countryside from the mosque, he could not hear it, or know that within the hour the night would end.

On catching sight of a man ahead, he left the road and hid behind a rock until the danger had passed. But then as he approached the town there began to be more people, so that he let himself down into the seguia, the deep ditch that went along beside the road. Here the stones and clumps of dead plants impeded his progress. He was still struggling along the floor of the seguia, pushing himself around the rocks and through the dry tangles of matted stalks left by the water, when dawn began to break.

The coming of daylight made him anxious and unhappy. He clambered up the bank of the seguia and raised his head to examine the road. A man walking past saw him, stood quite still, and then turned and ran back. Allal did not wait; he wanted now to get home as fast as possible.

Once he felt the thud of a stone as it struck the ground somewhere behind him. Quickly he threw himself over the edge of the seguia and rolled squirming down the bank. He knew the terrain here: where the road crossed the oued, there were two culverts not far apart. A man stood at some distance ahead of him with a shovel, peering down into the seguia. Allal kept moving, aware that he would reach the first culvert before the man could get to him.

The floor of the tunnel under the road was ribbed with hard little waves of sand. The smell of the mountains was in the air that moved through. There were places in here where he could have hidden, but he kept moving, and soon reached the other end. Then he continued to the second culvert and went under the road in the other direction, emerging once again into the seguia. Behind him several men had gathered at the entrance to the first culvert. One of them was on his knees, his head and shoulders inside the opening.

He now set out for the house in a straight line across the open ground, keeping his eye on the clump of palms beside it. The sun had just come up, and the stones began to cast long bluish shadows. All at once a small boy appeared from behind some nearby palms, saw him, and opened his eyes and mouth wide with fear. He was so close that Allal went straight to him and bit him in the leg. The boy ran wildly toward the group of men in the seguia.

Allal hurried on to the house, looking back only as he reached the hole between the mud bricks. Several men were running among the trees toward him. Swiftly he glided through into the alcove. The brown body still lay near the door. But there was no time, and Allal needed time to get back to it, to lie close to its head and say: Come here.

As he stared out into the room at the body, there was a great pounding on the door. The boy was on his feet at the first blow, as if a spring had been released, and Allal saw with despair the expression of total terror in his face, and the eyes with no mind behind them. The boy stood panting, his fists clenched. The door opened and some of the men peered inside. Then with a roar the boy lowered his head and rushed through the doorway. One of the men reached out to seize him, but lost his balance and fell. An instant later all of them turned and began to run through the palm grove after the naked figure.

Even when, from time to time, they lost sight of him, they could hear the screams, and then they would see him, between the palm trunks, still running. Finally he stumbled and fell face downward. It was then that they caught him, bound him, covered his nakedness, and took him away, to be sent one day soon to the hospital at Berrechid.

That afternoon the same group of men came to the house to carry out the search they had meant to make earlier. Allal lay in the alcove, dozing. When he awoke, they were already inside. He turned and crept to the hole. He saw the man waiting out there, a club in his hand.

The rage always had been in his heart; now it burst forth. As if his body were a whip, he sprang out into the room. The men nearest him were on their hands and knees, and Allal had the joy of pushing his fangs into two of them before a third severed his head with an axe.

Mejdoub

A man who spent his nights sleeping in cafés or under the trees or wherever he happened to be at the time when he felt sleepy, wandered one morning through the streets of the town. He came to the market place, where an old mejdoub dressed in rags cavorted before the populace, screaming prophecies into the air. He stood watching until the old man had finished and gathered up the money the people offered him. It astonished him to see how much the madman had collected, and having nothing else to do, he decided to follow him.

Almost before he got out of the market he was aware that small boys were hurrying from under the arcades to run alongside the mejdoub, who merely strode forward, chanting and waving his sceptre, and from time to time threatening the children who came too close. Walking at some distance behind, he saw the old man go into several shops. He came out each time with a banknote in his hand, which he promptly gave to one of the small boys.

It occurred to him then that there was much he could learn from this mejdoub. He had only to study the old man's behavior and listen carefully to the words he uttered. Then with practice he himself could make the same gestures and shout the same words. He began to look each day for the mejdoub and to follow him wherever he went in the town. At the end of a month he decided that he was ready to put his knowledge to use.

He travelled south to another city where he had never gone before. Here he took a very cheap room by the slaughterhouse, far from the centre of town. In the flea-market he bought an old and tattered djellaba. Then he went to the iron-mongers and stood watching while they made him a long sceptre like the one the mejdoub had carried.

The next day, after practicing for a while, he went into the town and sat down in the street at the foot of the largest mosque. For a while he merely looked at the people going past. Slowly he began to raise his arms to the sky, and then to gesture with them. No one paid him any attention. This reassured him, as it meant that his disguise was successful. When he began to shout words the passers-by looked toward him, but it was as if they could not see him, and were only waiting to hear what he had to say. For a time he shouted short quotations from the Koran. He moved his eyes in a circular motion and let his turban fall over his face. After crying the words *fire* and *blood* several times he lowered his arms and bent his head, and said no more. The people moved on, but not before many of them had tossed coins on the ground in front of him.

On succeeding days he tried other parts of the city. It did not seem to matter where he sat. The people were generous to him in one place the same as in another. He did not want to risk going into the shops and cafés until he was certain that the town had grown used to his presence. One day he stormed through the streets, shaking his sceptre to the sky and screaming: Sidi Rahal is here! Sidi Rahal tells you to prepare for the fire! This was in order to give himself a name for the townspeople to remember.

He began to stand in the doorways of shops. If he heard anyone refer to him as Sidi Rahal, he would step inside, glare at the proprietor, and without saying a word, hold out his hand. The man would give him money, and he would turn and walk out.

For some reason no children followed him. He would have been happier to have a group of them with him, like the old mejdoub, but as soon as he spoke to them, they were frightened and ran away. It's quieter like this, he told himself, but secretly it bothered him. Still, he was earning more money than he ever had thought possible. By the time the first rains arrived, he had saved up a large sum. Leaving his sceptre and ragged djellaba in his room by the slaughterhouse, he paid the landlord several months' rent in advance. He waited until night. Then he locked the door behind him and took a bus back to his own city.

First he bought a great variety of clothing. When he was richly dressed he went out and looked for a house. Soon he found one that suited him. It was small and he had enough money left to pay for it. He furnished two rooms and prepared to spend the winter eating and smoking kif with all his old friends.

When they asked him where he had been all summer, he spoke of the hospitality and generosity of his wealthy brother in Taza. Already he was impatient for the rains to stop. For there was no doubt that he truly enjoyed his new work.

The winter finally came to an end. He packed his bag and told his friends that he was going on a business trip. In the other town he walked to the room. His djellaba and sceptre were there.

This year many more people recognized him. He grew bolder and entered the shops without waiting in the doorways. The shopkeepers, eager to show their piety to the customers, always gave a good deal more than the passers-by.

One day he decided to make a test. He hailed a taxi. As he got in he bellowed: I must go to Sidi Larbi's tomb! Fast! The driver, who knew he was not going to be paid, nevertheless agreed, and they rode out to a grove of olive trees on a hill far from the town.

He told the driver to wait, and jumped out of the taxi. Then he began the long climb up the hill to the tomb. The driver lost patience and drove off. On the way back to the town he missed a curve and hit a tree. When he was let out of the hospital he spread the word that Sidi Rahal had caused the car to go off the road. Men talked at length about it, recalling other holy maniacs who had put spells on motors and brakes. The name of Sidi Rahal was on everyone's lips, and people listened respectfully to his rantings.

That summer he amassed more money than the year before. He returned home and bought a larger house to live in, while he rented out the first one. Each year he bought more houses and lands, until finally it was clear that he had become a very prosperous man.

Always when the first rains fell he would announce to his friends that he was about to travel abroad. Then he would leave secretly, never allowing anyone to see him off. He was delighted with the pattern of his life, and with the good luck he had been granted in being able to continue it. He assumed that Allah did not mind if he pretended to be one of His holy maniacs. The money was merely his reward for providing men with an opportunity to exercise their charity.

One winter a new government came to power and announced that all beggars were to be taken off the streets. He talked about this with his friends, all of whom thought it an excellent thing. He agreed with them, but the news kept him from sleeping at night. To risk everything by going back, merely because that was what he wanted to do, was out of the question. Sadly he resigned himself to spending the summer at home.

It was not until the first few weeks of spring had gone by that he realized how close it had been to his heart, the starting out on a fine starry night to go in the bus to the other city, and what a relief it had been each time to be able to forget everything and live as Sidi Rahal. Now he began to understand that his life here at home had been a pleasure only because he had known that at a certain moment he was going to leave it for the other life.

As the hot weather came on he grew increasingly restless. He was bored and lost his appetite. His friends, noticing the change in him, advised him to travel, as he always had done. They said that men had been known to die as a result of breaking a habit. Again he lay awake at night worrying, and then secretly he determined to go back. As soon as he had made the decision he felt much better. It was as though until then he had been asleep, and suddenly had awakened. He announced to his friends that he was going abroad.

That very night he locked up his house and got onto a bus. The next day he strode joyously through the streets to sit in his favorite spot by the mosque. Passers-by looked at him and remarked to one another: He's back again, after all. You see?

He sat there quietly all day, collecting money. At the end of the afternoon, since the weather was very hot, he walked down to the river outside the gates of the town, in order to bathe. As he was undressing behind some oleander bushes, he glanced up and saw three policemen coming down the bank toward him. Without waiting he seized his slippers, threw his djellaba over his shoulder, and began to run.

Sometimes he splashed into the water, and sometimes he slipped in the mud and fell. He could hear the men shouting after him. They did not chase him very far, for they were laughing. Not knowing this, he kept on running, following the river, until he was breathless and had to stop. He put on the djellaba and the slippers, thinking: I can't go back to the town, or to any other town, in these clothes.

He continued at a slower gait. When evening came he was hungry, but there were no people or houses in sight. He slept under a tree, with only the ragged djellaba to cover him.

The next morning his hunger had grown. He got up, bathed in the river, and set out again. All that day he walked under the hot sun. In the late afternoon he sat down to rest. He drank a little water from the river and looked around him at the countryside. On the hill behind him stood a partially ruined shrine.

When he was rested, he climbed up to the building. There was a tomb inside, in the center of the big domed room. He sat down and listened. Cocks crowed, and he heard the occasional barking of dogs. He imagined himself running to the village, crying to the first man he met: Give me a piece of bread, for the love of Moulay Abdelqader! He shut his eyes.

It was nearly twilight when he awoke. Outside the door stood a group of small boys, watching him. Seeing him awaken, they laughed and nudged one another. Then one boy tossed in a piece of dry bread, so that it fell beside him. Soon they were all chanting: He's eating bread! He's eating bread!

They played the game for a while, throwing in clods of earth and even uprooted plants along with the scraps of bread. In their faces he could read wonder, malice and contempt, and shining through these shifting emotions the steady gleam of ownership. He thought of the old mejdoub, and a shiver ran through him. Suddenly they had gone. He heard a few shrill cries in the distance as they raced back to the village.

The bread had given him a little nourishment. He slept where he was, and before it grew light he set out again along the river, giving thanks to Allah for having allowed him to get beyond the village without being seen. He understood that heretofore the children had run from him only because they knew that he was not ready for them, that they could not make him theirs. The more he thought

about this, the more fervently he hoped never to know what it was like to be a true mejdoub.

That afternoon as he turned a bend in the river, he came suddenly upon a town. His desperate need for food led him straight to the market, paying no heed to the people's stares. He went into a stall and ordered a bowl of soup. When he had finished it and paid, he entered another stall for a dish of stew. In a third place he ate skewered meat. Then he walked to the bread market for two loaves of bread to carry with him. While he was paying for these, a policeman tapped him on the shoulder and asked for his papers. He had none. There was nothing to say. At the police station they locked him into a small foul-smelling room in the cellar. Here in this closet he passed four days and nights of anguish. When at the end of that time they took him out and questioned him, he could not bring himself to tell them the truth. Instead he frowned, saying: I am Sidi Rahal.

They tied his hands and pushed him into the back of a truck. Later in the hospital they led him to a damp cell where the men stared and shivered and shrieked. He bore it for a week, and then he decided to give the officials his true name. But when he asked to be taken before them, the guards merely laughed. Sometimes they said: Next week, but usually they did not answer at all.

The months moved by. Through nights and days and nights he lived with the other madmen, and the time came when it scarcely mattered to him any more, getting to the officials to tell them who he was. Finally he ceased thinking about it.

You Have Left Your Lotus
Pods On The Bus

I soon learned not to go near the windows or to draw aside the double curtains in order to look at the river below. The view was wide and lively, with factories and warehouses on the far side of the Chao Phraya, and strings of barges being towed up and down through the dirty water. The new wing of the hotel had been built in the shape of an upright slab, so that the room was high and had no trees to shade it from the poisonous onslaught of the afternoon sun. The end of the day, rather than bringing respite, intensified the heat, for then the entire river was made of sunlight. With the redness of dusk everything out there became melodramatic and forbidding, and still the oven heat from outside leaked through the windows.

Brooks, teaching at Chulalongkorn University, was required as a Fulbright Fellow to attend regular classes in Thai; as an adjunct to this he arranged to spend much of his leisure time with Thais. One day he brought along with him three young men wearing the bright orange-yellow robes of Buddhist monks. They filed into the hotel room in silence and stood in a row as they were presented to me, each one responding by joining his palms together, thumbs touching his chest.

As we talked, Yamyong, the eldest, in his late twenties, explained that he was an ordained monk, while the other two were novices. Brooks then asked Prasert and Vichai if they would be ordained soon, but the monk answered for them.

"I do not think they are expecting to be ordained," he said quietly, looking at the floor, as if it were a sore subject all too often discussed among them. He glanced up at me and went on talking. "Your room is beautiful. We are not accustomed to such luxury." His voice was flat; he was trying to conceal his disapproval. The three conferred briefly in undertones. "My friends say they have never seen such a luxurious room," he reported, watching me closely through his steel-rimmed spectacles to see my reaction. I failed to hear.

They put down their brown paper parasols and their reticules that bulged with books and fruit. Then they got themselves into position in a row along the couch among the cushions. For a while they were busy adjusting the folds of their robes around their shoulders and legs.

"They make their own clothes," volunteered Brooks. "All the monks do."

I spoke of Ceylon; there the monks bought the robes all cut and ready to sew together. Yamyong smiled appreciatively and said: "We use the same system here."

The air-conditioning roared at one end of the room and the noise of boat motors on the river seeped through the windows at the other. I looked at the three sitting in front of me. They were very calm and self-possessed, but they seemed lacking in physical health. I was aware of the facial bones beneath their skin. Was the impression of sallowness partly due to the shaved eyebrows and hair?

Yamyong was speaking. "We appreciate the opportunity to use English. For this reason we are liking to have foreign friends. English, American; it doesn't matter. We can understand." Prasert and Vichai nodded.

Time went on, and we sat there, extending but not altering the subject of conversation. Occasionally I looked around the room. Before they had come in, it had been only a hotel room whose curtains must be kept drawn. Their presence and their comments on it had managed to invest it with a vaguely disturbing quality; I felt that they considered it a great mistake on my part to have chosen such a place in which to stay.

"Look at his tattoo," said Brooks. "Show him."

Yamyong pulled back his robe a bit from the shoulder, and I saw the two indigo lines of finely written Thai characters. "That is for good health," he said, glancing up at me. His smile seemed odd, but then, his facial expression did not complement his words at any point.

"Don't the Buddhists disapprove of tattooing?" I said.

"Some people say it is backwardness." Again he smiled. "Words for good health are said to be superstition. This was done by my abbot when I was a boy studying in the *wat*. Perhaps he did not know it was a superstition."

We were about to go with them to visit the *wat* where they lived. I pulled a tie from the closet and stood before the mirror arranging it.

"Sir," Yamyong began. "Will you please explain something? What is the significance of the necktie?"

"The significance of the necktie?" I turned to face him. "You mean, why do men wear neckties?"

"No. I know that. The purpose is to look like a gentleman."

I laughed. Yamyong was not put off. "I have noticed that some men wear the two ends equal, and some wear the wide end longer than the narrow, or the narrow longer than the wide. And the neckties themselves, they are not all the same length, are they? Some even with both ends equal reach below the waist. What are the different meanings?"

"There is no meaning," I said. "Absolutely none."

He looked to Brooks for confirmation, but Brooks was trying out his Thai on Prasert and Vichai, and so he was silent and thoughtful for a moment. "I believe you, of course," he said graciously. "But we all thought each way had a different significance attached."

As we went out of the hotel, the doorman bowed respectfully. Until now he had never given a sign that he was aware of my existence. The wearers of the yellow robe carry weight in Thailand.

A few Sundays later I agreed to go with Brooks and our friends to Ayudhaya. The idea of a Sunday outing is so repellent to me that deciding to take part in this one was to a certain extent a compulsive act. Ayudhaya lies less than fifty miles up the Chao Phraya from Bangkok. For historians and art-collectors it is more than just a provincial town; it is a period and a style—having been the Thai capital for more than four centuries. Very likely it still would be, had the Burmese not laid it waste in the eighteenth century.

Brooks came early to fetch me. Downstairs in the street stood the three bhikkus with their book bags and parasols. They hailed a cab, and without any previous price arrangement (the ordinary citizen tries to fix a sum beforehand) we got in and drove for twenty minutes or a half hour, until we got to a bus terminal on the northern outskirts of the city.

It was a nice, old-fashioned, open bus. Every part of it rattled, and the air from the rice fields blew across us as we pieced together our bits of synthetic conversation. Brooks, in high spirits, kept calling across to me: "Look! Water buffaloes!" As we went further away from Bangkok there were more of the beasts, and his cries became more frequent. Yamyong, sitting next to me, whispered: "Professor Brooks is fond of buffaloes?" I laughed and said I didn't think so.

"Then?"

I said that in America there were no buffaloes in the fields, and that was why Brooks was interested in seeing them. There were no temples in the landscape, either, I told him, and added, perhaps unwisely: "He looks at buffaloes. I look at temples." This struck Yamyong as hilarious, and he made allusions to it now and then all during the day.

The road stretched ahead, straight as a line in geometry, across the verdant, level land. Paralleling it on its eastern side was a fairly wide canal, here and there choked with patches of enormous pink lotuses. In places the flowers were gone and only the pods remained, thick green disks with the circular seeds embedded in their flesh. At the first stop the bhikkus got out. They came aboard again with mangosteens and lotus pods and insisted on giving us large numbers of each. The huge seeds popped out of the fibrous lotus cakes as though from a punchboard; they tasted almost like green almonds. "Something new for you today, I think," Yamyong said with a satisfied air.

Ayudhaya was hot, dusty, spread-out, its surrounding terrain strewn with ruins that scarcely showed through the vegetation. At some distance from the town there began a wide boulevard sparingly lined with important-looking buildings. It continued for a way and then came to an end as abrupt as its beginning. Growing up out of the scrub, and built of small russet-colored bricks, the ruined temples looked still unfinished rather than damaged by time. Repairs, done in smeared cement, veined their facades.

The bus's last stop was still two or three miles from the center of Ayudhaya. We got down into the dust, and Brooks declared: "The first thing we must do is find some food. They can't eat anything solid, you know, after midday."

"Not noon exactly," Yamyong said. "Maybe one o'clock or a little later."

"Even so, that doesn't leave much time," I told him. "It's quarter to twelve now."

But the bhikkus were not hungry. None of them had visited Ayudhaya before, and so they had compiled a list of things they most wanted to see. They spoke with a man who had a station wagon parked nearby, and we set off for a ruined *stupa* that lay some miles to the southwest. It had been built atop a high mound, which we climbed with some difficulty, so that Brooks could take pictures of us standing within a fissure in the decayed outer wall. The air stank of the bats that lived inside.

When we got back to the bus stop, the subject of food arose once again, but the excursion had put the bhikkus into such a state of excitement that they could not bear to allot time for anything but looking. We went to the museum. It was quiet; there were Khmer heads and documents inscribed in Pali. The day had begun to be painful. I told myself I had known beforehand that it would.

Then we went to a temple. I was impressed, not so much by the gigantic Buddha which all but filled the interior, as by the fact that not far from the entrance a man sat on the floor playing a *ranad* (pronounced *lanat*). Although I was familiar with the sound of it from listening to recordings of Siamese music, I had never before seen the instrument. There was a graduated series of wooden blocks strung together, the whole slung like a hammock over a boat-shaped resonating stand. The tones hurried after one another like drops of water falling very fast. After the painful heat outside, everything in the temple suddenly seemed a symbol of the concept of coolness—the stone floor under my bare feet, the breeze that moved through the shadowy interior, the bamboo fortune sticks being rattled in their long box by those praying at the altar, and the succession of insubstantial, glassy sounds that came from the *ranad*. I thought: If only I could get something to eat, I wouldn't mind the heat so much.

We got into the center of Ayudhaya a little after three o'clock. It was hot and noisy; the bhikkus had no idea of where to look for a restaurant, and the idea of asking did not appeal to them. The five of us walked aimlessly. I had come to the conclusion that neither Prasert nor Vichai understood spoken English, and I addressed myself earnestly to Yamyong. *"We've got to eat."* He stared at me with severity. "We are searching," he told me.

Eventually we found a Chinese restaurant on a corner of the principal street. There was a table full of boisterous Thais drinking *mekong* (categorized as whiskey, but with the taste of cheap rum) and another table occupied by an entire Chinese family. These people were doing some serious eating, their faces buried in their rice bowls. It cheered me to see them: I was faint, and had half expected to be told that there was no hot food available.

The large menu in English which was brought us must have been typed several decades ago and wiped with a damp rag once a week ever since. Under the heading SPECIALITIES were some dishes that caught my eye, and as I went through the list I began to laugh. Then I read it aloud to Brooks.

>*"Fried Sharks Fins and Bean Sprout*
>*Chicken Chins Stuffed with Shrimp*
>*Fried Rice Birds*
>*Shrimps Balls and Green Marrow*
>*Pigs Lights with Pickles*
>*Braked Rice Bird in Port Wine*
>*Fish Head and Bean Curd"*

Although it was natural for our friends not to join in the laughter, I felt that their silence was not merely failure to respond; it was heavy, positive.

A moment later three Pepsi-Cola bottles were brought and placed on the table. "What are you going to have?" Brooks asked Yamyong.

"Nothing, thank you," he said lightly. "This will be enough for us today."

"But this is terrible! You mean no one is going to eat *anything*?"

"You and your friend will eat your food," said

Yamyong. (He might as well have said "fodder.") Then he, Prasert, and Vichai stood up, and carrying their Pepsi-Cola bottles with them, went to sit at a table on the other side of the room. Now and then Yamyong smiled sternly across at us.

"I wish they'd stop watching us," Brooks said under his breath.

"They were the ones who kept putting it off," I reminded him. But I felt guilty, and I was annoyed at finding myself placed in the position of the self-indulgent unbeliever. It was almost as bad as eating in front of Moslems during Ramadan.

We finished our meal and set out immediately, following Yamyong's decision to visit a certain temple he wanted to see. The taxi drive led us through a region of thorny scrub. Here and there, in the shade of spreading flat-topped trees, were great round pits, full of dark water and crowded with buffaloes; only their wet snouts and horns were visible. Brooks was already crying: "Buffaloes! Hundreds of them!" He asked the taxi driver to stop so that he could photograph the animals.

"You will have buffaloes at the temple," said Yamyong. He was right; there was a muddy pit filled with them only a few hundred feet from the building. Brooks went and took his pictures while the bhikkus paid their routine visit to the shrine. I wandered into a courtyard where there was a long row of stone Buddhas. It is the custom of temple-goers to plaster little squares of gold leaf onto the religious statues in the *wats*. When thousands of them have been stuck onto the same surface, tiny scraps of the gold come unstuck. Then they tremble in the breeze, and the figure shimmers with a small, vibrant life of its own. I stood in the courtyard watching this quivering along the arms and torsos of the Buddhas, and I was reminded of the motion of the bô-tree's leaves. When I mentioned it to Yamyong in the taxi, I think he failed to understand, for he replied: "The bô-tree is a very great tree for Buddhists."

Brooks sat beside me on the bus going back to Bangkok. We spoke only now and then. After so many hours of resisting the heat, it was relaxing to sit and feel the relatively cool air that blew in from the rice fields. The driver of the bus was not a believer in cause and effect. He passed trucks with oncoming traffic in full view. I felt better with my eyes shut, and I might even have dozed off, had there not been in the back of the bus a man, obviously not in control, who was intent on making as much noise as possible. He began to shout, scream, and howl almost as soon as we had left Ayudhaya, and he did this consistently throughout the journey. Brooks and I laughed about it, conjecturing whether he was crazy or only drunk. The aisle was too crowded for me to be able to see him from where I sat. Occasionally I glanced at the other passengers. It was as though they were entirely unaware of the commotion behind them. As we drew closer to the city, the screams became louder and almost constant.

"God, why don't they throw him off?" Brooks was beginning to be annoyed.

"They don't even hear him," I said bitterly. People who can tolerate noise inspire me with envy and rage. Finally I leaned over and said to Yamyong: "That poor man back there! It's incredible!"

"Yes," he said over his shoulder. "He's very busy." This set me thinking what a civilized and tolerant people they were, and I marvelled at the sophistication of the word "busy" to describe what was going on in the back of the bus.

Finally we were in a taxi driving across Bangkok. I would be dropped at my hotel and Brooks would take the three bhikkus on to their *wat*. In my head I was still hearing the heartrending cries. What had the repeated word patterns meant?

I had not been able to give an acceptable answer to Yamyong in his bewilderment about the significance of the necktie, but perhaps he could satisfy my curiosity here.

"That man in the back of the bus, you know?"

Yamyong nodded. "He was working very hard, poor fellow. Sunday is a bad day."

I disregarded the nonsense. "What was he saying?"

"Oh, he was saying: 'Go into second gear,' or 'We are coming to a bridge,' or 'Be careful, people in the road.' Whatever he saw."

Since neither Brooks nor I appeared to have understood, he went on. "All the buses must have a driver's assistant. He watches the road and tells the driver how to drive. It is hard work because he must shout loud enough for the driver to hear him."

"But why doesn't he sit up in the front with the driver?"

"No, no. There must be one in the front and one in the back. That way two men are responsible for the bus."

It was an unconvincing explanation for the grueling sounds we had heard, but to show him that I believed him I said: "Aha! I see."

The taxi drew up in front of the hotel and I got out. When I said good-bye to Yamyong, he replied, I think with a shade of aggrievement: "Good-bye. You have left your lotus pods on the bus."

The Fqih

One midsummer afternoon a dog went running through a village, stopping just long enough to bite a young man who stood on the main street. It was not a deep wound, and the young man washed it at a fountain nearby and thought no more about it. However, several people who had seen the animal bite him mentioned it to his younger brother. You must take your brother to a doctor in the city, they said.

When the boy went home and suggested this, his brother merely laughed. The next day in the village the boy decided to consult the fqih. He found the old man sitting in the shade under the figtree in the courtyard of the mosque. He kissed his hand, and told him that a dog no one had ever seen before had bitten his brother and run away.

That's very bad, said the fqih. Have you got a stable you can lock him into? Put him there, but tie his hands behind him. No one must go near him, you understand?

The boy thanked the fqih and set out for home.

On the way he determined to cover a hammer with yarn and hit his brother on the back of the head. Knowing that his mother would never consent to seeing her son treated in this way, he decided that it would have to be done when she was away from the house.

That evening while the woman stood outside by the well, he crept up behind his brother and beat him with the hammer until he fell to the floor. Then he fastened his hands behind him and dragged him into a shed next to the house. There he left him lying on the ground, and went out, padlocking the door behind him.

When the brother came to his senses, he began a great outcry. The mother called to the boy: Quick! Run and see what's the matter with Mohammed. But the boy only said: I know what's the matter with him. A dog bit him, and the fqih said he has to stay in the shed.

The woman began to pull at her hair and scratch her face with her fingernails and beat her breasts. The boy tried to calm her, but she pushed him away and ran out to the shed. She put her ear to the door. All she could hear was her son's loud panting as he tried to free his hands from the cords that bound them. She pounded on the wood and screamed his name, but he was struggling, his face in the dirt, and did not reply. Finally the boy led her back to the house. It was written, he told her.

The next morning the woman got astride her donkey and rode to the village to see the fqih. He, however, had left that morning to visit his sister in Rhafsai, and no one knew when he would be back. And so she bought bread and started out on the road for Rhafsai, along with a group of villagers who were on their way to a souq in the region. That night she slept at the souq and the following morning at daybreak she started out again with a different group of people.

Each day the boy threw food in to his brother through a small barred window high above one of the stalls in the shed. The third day he also threw him a knife, so he could cut the ropes and use his hands to eat with. After a while it occurred to him that he had done a foolish thing in giving him the knife, since if he worked long enough with it he might succeed in cutting his way through the door. Thus he threatened to bring no more food until his brother had tossed the knife back through the window.

The mother had no sooner arrived at Rhafsai than she fell ill with a fever. The family with whom she had been travelling took her into their house and cared for her, but it was nearly a month before she was able to rise from the pallet on the floor where she had been lying. By that time the fqih had returned to his village.

Finally she was well enough to start out again. After two days of sitting on the back of the donkey she arrived home exhausted, and was greeted by the boy.

And your brother? she said, certain that by now he was dead.

The boy pointed to the shed, and she rushed to the door and began to call out to him.

Get the key and let me out! he cried.

I must see the fqih first, aoulidi. Tomorrow.

The next morning she and the boy went to the village. When the fqih saw the woman and her son come into the courtyard he raised his eyes to heaven. It was Allah's will that your son should die as he did, he told her.

But he's not dead! she cried. And he shouldn't stay in there any longer.

The fqih was astounded. Then he said: But let him out! Let him out! Allah has been merciful.

The boy however begged the fqih to come himself and open the door. So they set out, the fqih riding the donkey and the woman and boy following on foot. When they got to the shed, the boy handed the key to the old man, and he opened the door. The young man bounded out, followed by a stench so strong that the fqih shut the door again.

They went to the house, and the woman made tea for them. While they sat drinking, the fqih told the young man: Allah has spared you. You must never mistreat your brother for having shut you away. He did it on my orders.

The young man swore that never would he raise his hand against the boy. But the boy was still afraid, and could not bring himself to look at his brother. When the fqih left to return to the village, the boy went with him, in order to bring back the donkey. As they went along the road, he said to the old man: I'm afraid of Mohammed.

The fqih was displeased. Your brother is older than you, he said. You heard him swear not to touch you.

That night while they were eating, the woman went to the brazier to make the tea. For the first time the boy stole a glance at his brother, and grew cold with fear. Mohammed had swiftly bared his teeth and made a strange sound in his throat. He had done this as a kind of joke, but to the boy it meant something very different.

The fqih should never have let him out, he said to himself. Now he'll bite me, and I'll get sick like him. And the fqih will tell him to throw me into the shed.

He could not bring himself to look again at Mohammed. At night in the dark he lay thinking about it, and he could not sleep. Early in the morning he set out for the village, to catch the fqih before he began to teach the pupils at the msid.

What is it now? asked the fqih.

When the boy told him what he feared, the old man laughed. But he has no disease! He never had any disease, thanks to Allah.

But you yourself told me to lock him up, sidi.

Yes, yes. But Allah has been merciful. Now go home and forget about it. Your brother's not going to bite you.

The boy thanked the fqih and left. He walked through the village and out along the road that led finally to the highway. The next morning he got a ride in a truck that took him all the way to Casablanca. No one in the village ever heard of him again.

Istikhara, Anaya, Medagan and the Medaganat

In the Sahara, where the air, the light, even the sky suggest some as yet unvisited planet, it is not surprising to find certain patterns of human comportment equally unfamiliar. Behavior is strictly formulated, with little margin allowed for individual variations. If circumstances offer the opportunity for attack and pillage, the action is expected; indeed, custom demands it.

This is common knowledge. What may be less well-known are the two institutions of *istikhara* and *anaya*. The first is an invocation, offered up just before going to sleep, in which the supplicant implores Allah to send a dream which will make it possible for him to solve his difficulties. The prayer must be uttered in full four times over before the request is made for the specific revelatory details that will determine the sleeper's course of action when he awakens. The orison may or may not be answered. It is up to the supplicant to decide whether his dream is a result of *istikhara* or not, and, if it seems to him that it is, to interpret its material correctly. The practice seems a sound one: not only does it assume that dreams can be therapeutic, but it offers Moslems a practical technique for producing them.

Anaya, on the other hand, is a custom devoid of meaning save in a feudal society. It is the last feeble hope left to a soldier defeated in battle. If he can manage to crawl to one of the enemy and get his head totally under the folds of the other's burnous, he is automatically saved from death. His pardon, however, involves him with the wearer of the burnous for the rest of his life, or until the wearer dies. He becomes his enemy's permanent possession and responsibility. At the time when the events cited here took place, which is to say roughly a hundred years ago, *anaya* still functioned as an integral part of Saharan military etiquette.

A man named Medagan appeared one day in Ouargla, accompanied by seven of his sons. They sat with the Chaamba and told them of how for some misdemeanor or other their own tribe of Kelkhela Tuareg had driven them out of their homeland in the Hoggar, and how they had wandered and suffered ever since. The Chaamba listened and took them in to live with them. First they lent them some of their camels, and later let them have large quantities of dates and wheat on credit. This gave the Tuareg the mobility they seemed to require. For several months they lived in the vicinity of Ouargla, hunting and getting themselves into good health. Then they went back to Ouargla and robbed the Chaamba of twenty of their best camels, which they proceeded to drive off into an uninhabited region. There, hidden in the deep ravines of the desolate Tademait country, they lived for two years or more, moving out of their lair only to attack caravans that passed nearby. At length, apparently considering themselves invulnerable, they had the audacity to ride up to the very gates of El Golea and capture thirty camels from under the eyes of the Chaamba who owned them.

A Chaambi from Ouargla happened to be with the other Chaamba when the raid took place. He was one of those who had been willing to give Medagan wheat on credit. When he had finished telling the others that part of the story, the men determined to go in pursuit of the Tuareg. A few days later sixty men set out on fast *mehara*.

When Medagan and his sons arrived back at their hiding place they suspected that they might be followed, but they were fairly confident that the Chaamba would not venture into the maze of gorges and narrow passageways which characterize the terrain. Nevertheless, before lying down to sleep that night, Medagan prayed for a dream that could guide his behavior in the event the Chaamba did manage to catch up with them. In the morning when he awoke and realized with dismay that he had had no dream whatever, or none that he could recall, he conferred with his sons. They read this as an unfavorable omen, and agreed that if they were forced into battle they would seek *anaya*, throwing themselves upon the mercy of the Chaamba once again, this time definitively. Then Medagan sent off his youngest son, who was no more than a child, with some camels they had captured earlier, to sell them in El Golea. Since the group had just returned from there, this act would seem to indicate that Medagan foresaw the possibility of serious trouble, and hoped to save this son at least. In this he was successful, for the boy reached El Golea with the camels, unharmed.

The Chaamba meanwhile found the group with ease, and heard Medagan call out to them that Allah had advised him to seek *anaya*. Seeing that the Tuareg in truth were not even attempting to defend themselves, the Chaamba settled the matter by sending their black slaves against them. This ruled out the possibility of *anaya*, since a slave is powerless to grant it. The blacks cut the throat of each man, thus ending the saga of Medagan and his sons.

This took place in 1863, just as the French were making strenuous efforts to extend their hegemony southward into the desert. It marked the beginning of a twenty-year period of excessive lawlessness throughout the Sahara. Bandit groups sprang up on all sides to sweep down on oases, plunder passing caravans, and massacre voyagers. Some of this activity was legitimate retaliation for French incursions, but the greater part was simple outlawry, due no doubt to the breakdown in moral conventions attendant upon the prolonged infidel presence.

A small group of the Mekhadema tribe having been attacked and murdered in the same region of the Tademait where Medagan had met his death, the popular imagination around Ouargla was quick to attribute the raid to Medagan and his sons, who were declared to be wreaking vengeance from beyond the grave in return for having been denied the possibility of *anaya* by the Chaamba. Thereafter, as the raids proliferated, each new *razzia* was attributed to the ghosts of the Medaganat, and the word fast came to be a Saharan synonym for outlaw. Every petty thief, agitator, pillager, renegade or highwayman was labeled a Medagani. Only the empty shell of the word remained, its original and secondary meanings both having been lost in the general confusion that existed in the region. The assaults became organized and took on a more openly political character. Now it was the Chaamba themselves en masse who decided to be outlaws, and who in 1871 adopted the name of Medaganat as their official designation.

In 1876 they boasted of killing the three French priests, Fathers Paulmier, Menoret, and Boujard. The French press reacted with hysteria: the situation in the Sahara was utterly intolerable. Meanwhile the attacks increased in number and violence. The Medaganat conducted raids along the Tunisian border, in Libya, in Morocco, and throughout the Algerian desert. It was only several years later, in 1883, when they were careless enough to attack a group of Reguibat, that they finally met with an enemy able to destroy them.

At the very beginning of the battle a good many of the Medaganat, sensing likely defeat, defected outright to the Reguibat. The others, once it became clear that they could not win, then tried like their original namesakes to obtain *anaya*. But the women of the Reguibat, who were with them in the camp, repeatedly warned their menfolk not to grant it. Thus the Reguibat were obliged to chop the Medaganat into pieces with their swords to prevent them from touching the folds of their capes. The women furthermore insisted that even those who had surrendered at the outset be slaughtered. This was a grave infraction of desert law, but to oblige them the men cut a few dozen throats, and finally the women were quiet.

In this instance it is clear that neither *anaya* nor

istikhara produced what was desired of it, and yet the results were by no means the same as they would have been had neither been practiced. To a Moslem, the failure of Medagan's attempt at *istikhara* is implicit in the facts. One may pray, but if one is not in a state of grace the prayer fails to get through. Once Medagan had betrayed his protectors, he was not in a condition which permitted contact with the Deity. And having construed his dreamless night as an instruction to seek *anaya*, by going out and requesting it immediately, without making even a gesture of self-defense, he doubtless helped to bring about his own defeat. To the Chaamba this behavior could only have seemed a proof of cowardice; the sending of slaves to despatch the bandits thus gave a flavor of contempt to their refusal. Apparently, Medagan and his sons were beyond the radius of normal functioning with regard to both *istikhara* and *anaya*. Many of the Chaamba Medaganat, however, would have been saved by *anaya* if the Reguibat had not happened to have their women along.

Thus there was no *istikhara*, no *anaya*, Medagan was not a Medagani, and the Medaganat had never heard of Medagan.

The Waters of Izli

No one would have guessed, from seeing the two villages spread out there, one higher up than the other on the sunny slope of the mountain, that enmity existed between them. And yet, if you looked closely, you would see certain marked differences in the respective designs they made on the landscape. Tamlat was higher, the houses were farther apart, and there were trees between them. In Izli everything was crowded together, for there was not enough space. The entire village seemed to have been built on top of boulders and at the edges of cliffs. Green fields and meadows surrounded Tamlat. It lay above, where the valley was wide, so that there was ample room for farming, and thus the people lived well. But the orchards down in Izli were little more than steep stairways of terraces. No matter how hard they worked trying to raise vegetables and fruit, the villagers never had enough.

What ought to have helped compensate for Izli's unlucky site was the large spring just outside the village, whose water was the sweetest in the region. The people of Izli claimed great curative powers for it, an idea that was dismissed by the inhabitants of Tamlat, although they themselves often went down and filled their skins and jars with it to take home with them. There was no way of fencing off the land around the spring, or the natives of Izli long ago would have seen to it that no one else had access to the water. If only the people of Tamlat had been willing to admit that the water was superior to their own, eventually they might have been persuaded to trade a few vegetables for it. However, they were careful never to mention it, and except for going casually to fetch it, behaved as if it did not exist.

The man whose land lay nearest to the spring was Ramadi, said to be the most prosperous one in Izli. By the standards of Tamlat he would not have been considered well-off. But his black mare was the only horse in Izli, and his orchard had twenty-three almond trees growing on eight different levels, and on each level he had built a channel that ran with clear water. The mare was a beautiful animal, and he kept her in perfect condition. When he dressed in his white selham and rode the mare through the street out of the village, the people of Izli remarked to each other that he looked almost like Sidi Bouhajja. This was a great compliment, since Sidi Bouhajja was the most important saint in the region. He too wore white garments and rode a black horse, although his was a stallion.

For a long time Ramadi had been on the lookout for a fitting mate for his mare. However, not one stallion among all those he had looked at in the neighboring villages could be called her equal. In fact, the only horse he would have accepted for her was the shining black stallion ridden by Sidi Bouhajja, and this was out of the question, since there was no way of asking a saint for such a favor.

It was assumed by many people that Sidi Bouhajja and his horse were able to converse together. And it was common knowledge, for he had proclaimed it in public on several occasions, that at the moment of his death it was to be the horse that would decide on his burial place. He asked that his body be fastened astride the animal, which was then to be allowed to go where it pleased. Where it stopped, at that spot Sidi Bouhajja was to be interred. This doubtless lent weight to the belief that the old man and his horse had a secret language between them.

It was a subject for much speculation around the countryside as to which region might prove fortunate enough to witness this event, but everything was cut short by Sidi Bouhajja's sudden collapse one afternoon as he sat outside the mosque at Tamlat.

The saint had ridden up through Izli earlier in the day, passing by Ramadi's house as the mare stood in front of it, shaded by an old olive tree. The stallion wanted to stop, and Sidi Bouhajja had some difficulty in getting him to continue. Ramadi watched, fingering his beard, thinking what a great thing it would be if the stallion should suddenly rise up, saint and all, and mount the mare. Then, feeling ashamed, he looked away.

Later in the day Ramadi got onto the mare and rode up to Tamlat. There in a corner of the market he caught sight of an Aissaoui snake charmer from Izli whom he knew, and he sat down to talk with him. It was then that he heard the news of Sidi

Bouhajja's death.

He sat up very straight. The Aissaoui added that soon they would be tying the saint to his horse.

Where do you think it'll go? Ramadi asked him.

It'll probably come here and go into the grain market, the Aissaoui said.

Have you got your snakes with you?

The Aissaoui looked surprised. Yes, I have them, he said.

Get them out there to the turn-off and let him see them, Ramadi told him. He's got to go down the hill instead.

He rose, jumped onto his mare, and rode off.

The Aissaoui ran to the fondouq where he had left his basket of vipers and cobras. Then he hurried up to the corner where the road turned off from the main street and led down the side of the mountain.

Since everyone in Tamlat was watching the elders strap Sidi Bouhajja's body onto the back of the stallion, Ramadi on his mare passed unnoticed as he galloped down the road to Izli. When he got to his house, he left the mare standing under the olive tree and waited.

Up in Tamlat the Assaoui sat by the edge of the road with his basket. At length he saw the horse come into view, its sacred burden strapped to its back. It cantered down the street toward him, followed at some distance by the elders. He opened his basket and took out two of the larger serpents, holding one in each hand. As the horse approached him, he stood up and made the reptiles writhe in the air. Immediately the horse opened its eyes very wide and turned to the right, down the road leading out of the village.

The Aissaoui put the snakes back into the basket

and sauntered out of the bushes which until then had hidden him from the approaching elders. They paid him no attention, and he set out along the road to Izli. Far ahead of him he could see the black form of the stallion racing down the mountainside, the white bundle it carried flopping in the sunlight. After he had walked along for a while, he turned to look back. The elders stood up there at the corner, shading their eyes as they peered down into the valley.

And as Ramadi sat in his doorway waiting, the stallion stormed into the village, stood quiet for an instant, and then trotted directly to Ramadi's house. The mare still stood under the olive tree, switching her tail against the flies. Before anyone arrived to watch, the stallion reared himself up to a great height, bursting the straps that had bound Sidi Bouhajja to his back. The body in the white selham dropped to the ground at the same moment the stallion seized the mare. Ramadi ran forward and pulled it out of the way. Then he returned to the doorway to look on.

A little later some neighbors arrived, and they carried Sidi Bouhajja into Ramadi's courtyard, all the while praising Allah. By the time the men of Tamlat had got down to Izli, the stallion and the mare were standing quietly under the olive tree, and the tolba of Izli chanted inside Ramadi's house.

The men from Tamlat hid their chagrin and accepted the will of Allah. The horse had come to Izli and stopped here, therefore this was where Sidi Bouhajja had to be buried. They helped the men of Izli dig the grave, and the news went out to all the villages around, so that tolba came from many places to chant at the tomb.

It was no time before crowds of pilgrims began to arrive in Izli, seeking baraka at Sidi Bouhajja's tomb. Soon it was necessary to demolish Ramadi's house and in its place to build a sanctuary where the pilgrims could sleep. At the same time they constructed a domed qoubba over the saint's resting place by the olive tree, and then built a high wall around it. Ramadi was given another house nearby.

Since the pilgrims all carried away with them water from the spring, the water's fame soon spread, and it took on great importance. Even those who did not venerate Sidi Bouhajja came to drink it and take it home with them. In exchange they left offerings of food and money in the sanctuary. Before a year was up, Izli had become more prosperous than Tamlat.

Only Ramadi and the Aissaoui knew of the part they had played in bringing about the stroke of good luck that had changed their village, and they considered it of slight importance, since everything is decided by Allah. What mattered to Ramadi was the beauty of the black colt that now followed the mare wherever he rode her, even if it was down to the plain or up to the market in Tamlat.

Afternoon With Antaeus

You wanted to see me? They told you right. That's my name. Ntiuz. The African Giant's what they've called me ever since I started fighting. What can I do for you? Have you seen the town? It isn't such a bad place. You're lucky the wind's not blowing these days. We have a bad wind that comes through here. But without it the sun's too hot. Argos? Never heard of it. I've never been over to the other side.

A man named Erakli? Yes, yes, he was here. It was a long time ago. I remember him. We even put on a fight together.

Killed me! Is that what he told them back there? I see. And when you got here you heard I was still around, and so you wanted to meet me? I understand.

Why don't we sit here? There's a spring in the courtyard that has the coldest water in town. You asked about Erakli. No, he had no trouble here, except losing his fight. Why would anyone bother him? A man alone. You never saw him before. You let him go on his way. You don't bother him. Only savages attack a stranger walking alone. They kill him and fight over his loincloth. We let people go through without a word. They come in on one side and go out on the other. That's the way we like it. Peaceful and friendly with everyone. We have a saying: Never hit a man unless you know you can kill him, and then kill him fast. Up where I come from we're rougher than they are down here on the coast. We have a harder life, but we're healthier. Look at me, and I could almost be your father. If I'd lived down here on the coast all my life I wouldn't be like this now. And still I'm nothing to what I was twenty years ago. In those days I went to every festival and put on shows for the people. I'd lift a bull with one hand and hit him between the horns with the other, so he'd fall dead. People like to see that. Sometimes I broke beams with my head. That was popular, too, but the bull was religious, of course, so it was the one people wanted to see most. There was nobody who didn't know about me.

Have some nuts? I eat them all day. I get them up in the forest. There are trees up there bigger than any you ever saw.

It was at least twenty years ago he came through here, but I remember him, all right. Not because he was any good as a fighter, but because he was so crazy. You can't help remembering a man as crazy as Erakli.

Have some more. I've got a whole sack full. That's true, the flavor's not quite like anything else. I don't suppose you have them over on the other side.

I'll be only too glad to take you up to the forest, if you'd like to see it. It's not far. You don't mind climbing a little?

Of course he didn't make any friends here, but a man like that can't have friends. He was so full of great ideas about himself that he didn't even see us. He thought we were all savages, ready to swallow his stories. Even before the fight everybody was laughing at him. Strong, yes, but not a good fighter. An awful boaster and a terrible liar. And ignorant.

We'll turn here and go up this path. He talked all the time. If you believed him, there was nothing he couldn't do, and do it better than anybody else.

You'll get a fine view on the way. The edge of the world. How does it feel, when you're used to being in the middle, to be out here at the end? It must be a different feeling.

Erakli came into town without anyone noticing him. He must have had a little money with him, because he began to meet two or three men I knew every day and pay for their drinks. They told me about him, and I went along one day just to see what he looked like, not to meet him. Right away I knew he was no good. No good as a fighter, no good as a man. I didn't even take him seriously enough to challenge him. How can you take a man seriously when he has a beard that looks like the wool on a sheep?

He stayed around town a while and saw me kill a few bulls. I fought a match or two, too, while he was here, and it seems he came each time to watch me. The next thing I knew, he'd challenged me. It was he who wanted the match. It was hard to believe. And what's more, they told me he held it against me that I hadn't been the one who challenged him. It just never entered my mind.

All this land you see up here is mine. This and the forest up ahead. I keep everybody out. I like to walk, and I don't want to meet people while I'm walking. It makes me nervous. I used to fight every man I met. At least, in the beginning.

When I was a small boy in my village I liked to go late in the afternoon to a big rock. I'd sit on it and look down the valley and pretend enemies were coming. I'd let them get to a certain point, and then I'd start a boulder rolling down the mountain to hit them. I killed them every time. My father caught me and I got punished. I might have hit sheep or goats, or even men down there.

But I'm not dead, as you can see, no matter what Erakli may be saying. I want you to look at my trees. Look at the size of the trunk of that one. Follow it up, up, up, to where the first branches begin. Have you ever seen trees this big anywhere?

When I got a little older I learned how to throw a calf, and later a bull. By that time I was fighting. Never lost yet. They forgot my name was Ntiuz and began to call me The Giant. Not because of my size, of course. I'm not so big. But because nobody could beat me in a match. They came from all around, and afterwards from far away. You know how they do when they hear of a fighter who's never lost. They can't believe that somehow or other they won't manage to get him down. That was the way with your Erakli. I didn't meet him until the fight, but I'd heard all about him from my friends. He told them he'd studied me, and he knew how to beat me. He didn't say how he was going to do it. And I never even found out what he thought he was going to do until after the fight.

No, I'm not dead. I'm still the champion. Anybody here can tell you. It's too bad you never met Erakli yourself. You wouldn't be so surprised. You'd understand that whatever he said when he got back home was what he wanted to tell and nothing more. He couldn't tell the truth if he wanted to.

Are you tired? It's a steep climb if you're not used to it. The fight itself? It didn't last long. He was so busy trying to use the system he'd worked out. He'd back away, and then come up to me and just stand there with his hands on me. I couldn't understand what he was trying to do. The crowd was jeering. For a minute I thought: He's the kind that gets his pleasure this way, running his hands over a man's chest and squeezing his waist. He didn't like it because I laughed and shouted to the crowd. He was very serious the whole time. And I was wrong anyway. Are we going too fast? And you're carrying that heavy pouch at your waist. We can go as slowly as you want to. There's no hurry.

That's a good idea. Why don't we sit a minute and rest? Do you feel all right? No. Nothing. I thought you looked a little pale. It may be the light. The sun never gets down in here.

It was only after the fight that one of my friends told me what Erakli wanted to do. Instead of trying to throw me, the crazy fool was trying to lift me off the ground and hold me in the air! Not so he could throw me down better, but just to hold me up there. It's hard to believe, isn't it? But that's what he had in his mind. That was his great system. Why? Don't ask me. I'm an African. I don't know what goes on in the heads of the men of your country.

Have some more nuts. No, no, they couldn't have hurt you. It's the air. Our climate doesn't suit people from the other side. While he was trying to make up his mind how to lift me I finished him. They had to drag him out.

Shall we go on? Or would you rather wait a while? Are you still out of breath? There's no air here in the forest.

Don't you think we ought to wait a while? Of course, if you want to go. We can walk slowly. Let me help you up. It's too bad we couldn't have gone further. The biggest trees are up that way.

Yes, they dragged him out, and he stayed three days lying on a mat before he left here. Finally he limped out of town like a dog, with everybody laughing at him along the way. Hang on to me. I won't let you fall. You're walking all right. Just keep going. He didn't look left or right on his way out of town. Must have been glad to get into the mountains.

Relax. First one foot, then the other foot. I don't know where he went. I'm afraid there's no water here. We'll get some as soon as we get to town. You'll be all right. I suppose he went back where he came from. We never saw him again here, in any case.

Does it seem like such a long time that we've been walking? It's only a few minutes. You recognize the path but you don't know where you are? Why should you know where you are? It's not your forest. Relax. Step. Step. Step.

You're right. It's the rock where we were sitting a few minutes ago. I wondered if you'd notice. Of course I know my way! I thought you'd better rest again before we started into town. That's right, you just lie back there. You'll be fine as soon as you've had a little sleep. It's very quiet here.

No, you haven't been asleep so long. How do you feel now? Good. I knew a little sleep would do it.

You're not used to the air here. A pouch? I don't think you were carrying anything.

There's no need to make a face like that. You don't think I took it, do you?

I thought we were friends. I treated you like a friend. And now you pay me back.

I'm not going to take you anywhere. Get down to the town by yourself. I'm going the other way.

Go on back to your country and tell them about me. You can walk all right.

Just keep going.

And get out of the forest fast!

Reminders of Bouselham

When I was a boy, Mother's favorite spot for reading, the place where she sat when she was going to read for a long time, was an old chaise longue, kept always in the same position in a corner of the east room, far enough from the walls so that the light came in over her shoulders on both sides. The back of the chaise longue was piled with dozens of small down-stuffed cushions. It was a comfortable seat to recline in. Sometimes I would use it for a few minutes in the morning before she was up. Once she caught me there and ridiculed me.

Getting decrepit in your old age! she scoffed. You're a growing boy. That's a chair for an adult.

The garden was the place to lie on a summer afternoon. Overhead the wind hissed in the high eucalyptus and cypress trees. There were flying skeins of fog that swept by very fast, just above, sometimes catching the tops of the trees and swooping down through the branches. One summer when I was back from school in England I did all my studying out there on the ground behind bushes or hedges, or anywhere that was hidden from the sight of the house.

And I would lie face-down in the hot garden, and look beneath the cut tips of the grass spears, into the miniature forest where the ants lived. Most of them were very small, and were not troubled by the mat I spread out over their domain. If the large red ones discovered it, as now and then they did, they attacked at once, and there was nothing to do but carry the mat somewhere else.

It went without saying that the Medina was forbidden territory. Mother would have reacted very badly had she known I had ever been in it alone. But from time to time I went on an errand and had the opportunity to slip into the old town and find my way along the alleys for a few minutes. I loved the way they suddenly changed direction and burrowed under the houses. In fact, you went under a house to get into the alley where Mama Tiemponada's brothel stood. Hers was not the only one there, but it was the biggest. All the houses in the alley were brothels. The women leaned in the doorways and made remarks to the men walking by. I found the place mysterious and sinister. It seemed natural enough that Mother should not want me to come to the Medina.

One evening as I stood outside Mama Tiemponada's in the alley watching the door, it opened and a single Moroccan boy came out. He stood still for an instant, and looking up at the full moon directly above, whistled once at it, then walked away. This struck me as very strange, and I remembered it. The whistle was casual and intimate, suggesting that the moon and he had been good friends for a long time.

A year or two later, when Bouselham came to work for us, I thought I recognized him as the same boy.

Probably it would have been better for me if I'd got to know Father, but I never did. It did not occur to me to wonder what sort of man he was. His fiftieth birthday was well behind him when I was born, and by then he was interested primarily in golf. He paid no attention to me, and very little to Mother. At daybreak he would get up, eat a big breakfast, and ride his favorite horse to the country club at Boubana. We would not see him again until evening. The ladies said to Mother: Colonel Driscoll is so impressive up there on his horse! Their own husbands drove in their cars to the country club. I was convinced that they were secretly laughing at us because Father was so odd.

As a boy I sometimes played with Amy, because she lived on the property next to ours, down the road. She was five years older than I, a tomboy, and full of sadistic impulses which she often vented on me. When she was twenty her mother died, and Amy was left alone in a house far too big for her. Then she began to spend almost all her time with Mother.

I was not surprised when Mother announced casually one day: Amy has a buyer for Villa Vireval. She's coming to stay with us for a while.

Soon Amy was with us. She had changed with the years, and was now an introverted, nervous young woman with a passion for precision. She had an annoying tic: the constantly repeated clearing of her throat. In the beginning Father made an effort to converse with her, even though he was very much against having her with us. She was neurotic, he said; she was morbid and self-centered, and she sapped Mother's energy.

What's wrong with that girl? Can't she leave you alone for a minute?

Mother, who like anyone else enjoyed being admired, was grateful even for Amy's devotion.

She's a well-balanced girl. I can't think what you have against her.

As usual the gossip got the basic facts fairly straight, but the motivations wrong. Everyone was certain that Father had left home because of Bouselham, when actually it was because he could no longer bear to be in the same house with Amy. He put up with her for six months. Then, seeing that she had no intention of leaving, and that Mother was adamant in her refusal to suggest to her that she find another place to live, he suddenly went off to Italy. Mother was unperturbed. Your father needs a holiday, she said to me after he had gone. Of course she assumed he would return.

It was precisely at that point that Bouselham emerged from his obscurity. Father had engaged him a year or so earlier, when he was sixteen, as an assistant gardener. He weeded, raked, and carried water in the lower garden, and one seldom saw him anywhere near the house. But when Father left, he began to come into the kitchen, where the maids would give him tea. Before long he was eating regularly there with them, rather than sitting under a tree with whatever he had brought with him from home.

How did the relationship start between him and Mother? What was the beginning of it? There is no way of bringing up the subject with Bouselham, since it has never been mentioned and thus does not exist between us. But I know that whatever the beginning may have been, it was Mother who set it in motion.

Often Bouselham had nothing to do but sit in a café smoking kif, and it was not always certain that there would be someone who could play cards with him. Most men worked during the day and came into the café after they had finished. Bouselham did not have to work. Ever since the colonel had gone away he had been with the colonel's wife. She did not want him to work, because then he would have to get up very early every morning, whereas she liked to sleep late and have him with her. All the men in the café knew that Bouselham had a rich Nazarene woman who gave him whatever he wanted.

And this was what Amy eventually began to say to Mother in one way or another, over and over. In her view it was wrong of Mother to have Bouselham with her, not only because his culture, religion and social class were not hers, but also because he was too young for a woman of her age. Usually Mother replied blandly that she didn't agree, but now and then she said a bit more. I heard her say one day: You're trying to encroach on my private life, Amy, and you have no right to.

Not too long after that, Amy decided to go to Paris where a friend had invited her. She packed up very quickly and was suddenly gone. Mother limited her comment to saying: Amy's a very sweet girl who has everything to learn, I'm afraid. And whether she will or not, I wonder.

The day Amy left I wandered into her room and looked around. It needed a thorough cleaning. I pulled the bureau out from the wall and peered down behind it. Underneath, wedged behind a back leg, was a crumpled postcard-size glossy print of Bouselham in bathing trunks on the beach at Sidi Qanqouch. For me this put Amy's quarrel with Mother in a new light. For a moment I was even sorry she was gone; it would have been fun to see what a few leading questions might have brought out from behind those thin precise lips of hers. Had she coveted Bouselham for herself? Or did Mother interrupt something that was already going on between them when she brought Bouselham into the house to sleep in her room?

The tale had been going around Tangier for many months. I heard it first from an English woman; she had just arrived here, and so had no way of knowing that the subject of her story was my mother. The colonel's wife used to disappear every night into the dark corners of the garden to meet the gardener, who was no more than a boy, an ordinary Moroccan workman. And when the colonel had had enough of her nonsense he had left, whereupon she had calmly taken the servant into the house and lived with him. I'm told she's even given him a racing car! she added, pretending to burst into laughter.

Probably, I said.

There is no doubt that Mother changed in certain respects during the time Bouselham was living in the house. She did buy a second-hand Porsche convertible for him, and this was certainly most unlike her. Her manner became distant; she seemed uninvolved in all the things that heretofore had been her life. When I suggested that I move out of the house and take a flat in town, she merely raised her eyebrows. You'll come to dinner twice a week, was all she said.

What finally decided her against Bouselham was a long and complicated saga involving his sister. Once she had carefully checked on the details of the story, her resolve to get rid of him was instantaneous. However, the only way she could devise for accomplishing this was so drastic as to be laughable. Mother has lived in this country for many years, and should not have been so deeply disturbed by Bouselham's behavior, particularly since it had nothing whatever to do with her. To me what he did seems natural enough, but then, I was born here. I first heard about it from Bouselham himself, not long after I moved out of the house and took the apartment in town.

I had been out to dinner and had walked home afterward. A thunderstorm was approaching from the direction of the strait. Soon hail showered against the windows. There was a very bright bolt of lightning, and the electricity was gone. I got out a flashlight, started some candles burning, and stood in front of the fireplace for a while. The thunderstorm circled around and came back, and it rained harder. In the midst of this there was a banging on the door, and when I opened it I found Bouselham standing there, completely wet.

He looked as wild and as pleased with himself as ever, in spite of the rivulets of rain running down his face. Immediately he took off his shoes and socks and crouched in front of the fireplace, almost inside it, while he talked. Every day, he said, he was seeing a lawyer friend of his who was helping him.

To do what? I asked.

Avoiding a direct answer, he pivoted on his heels to face me, and asked if I could let him have ten thousand francs. The lawyer had to have the money for photocopies and notarizations. His fee would be contingent upon the success of his case, later. As soon as I had agreed to let him have the money, the story began to come out.

A certain rich merchant of the Medina, intent on the pleasures of the twilight hour, used to go each day and sit in a café at the end of the city. Here he could see in three directions, and hundreds of people were visible nearby and in the distance, walking along the roads. Each day, sooner or later, a girl passed by with an older woman who carried a basket. He sat at a table on the sidewalk, facing in the direction from which they always came, so that he could see them from far away, and watch the girl as she approached. Every afternoon he saw her eyes pick him out from among the others at the café, but from that moment on she would give no sign of knowing he was there.

How many years since I've seen such a beauty? he sighed. He would notice them coming far down the road under the eucalyptus trees, long before she could see him, for they were walking into the sunset light. The instant came when she saw him, and then her head bent forward. The rich merchant would watch her as she came nearer, his eyes never leaving her. It seemed to him that she was dancing rather than walking, and as she went past, often so near that he could have touched her djellaba by stretching out his arm, he was exasperated by the impossibility of speaking with her.

Maybe one day they'll let her out by herself, he thought, and so he waited.

The day finally came when he saw her walking along carrying the basket herself, and no one was with her. Ah, he said softly, rubbing the ends of his fingers together. He called the waiter and paid him. Then he sat quietly until she had gone by. As the girl turned the corner he got up and began to walk after her.

He caught up with her only after she had gone into another street. May I drive you somewhere? he asked her.

You may drive me home if you like, she said.

This was not what the rich merchant had hoped to hear. However, he led her to his car, which was parked not far away.

I brought Bouselham a cup of coffee. He sipped it, still crouching by the fire, and said nothing for several minutes. Then abandoning his story-telling manner, he went on casually, as though recapitulating a tale I already knew.

And I was just coming out of a bacal there, and I saw this Mercedes parked up ahead. And not with Belgian license-plates, either. Moroccan ones, and that means money. And then, while I was still looking, I stopped believing what I was seeing, because the door of the car opened and my sister got out and ran up toward the corner. I knew she'd seen me and didn't think I'd seen her. The first thing I thought of was going after her and killing her. While I stood there the car drove away. I didn't see the man or get the number.

What good would that have done, if you'd killed her? I said, although I knew that for him it was one of those meaningless European remarks. Surprisingly, he laughed and said: I'm not that stupid. I felt sorry for her, though, that night when I got her alone at home and saw how frightened she was.

I saw you get out of the car, I told her. But then I said: You say he's always at the Café Dakhla. Tomorrow you're going to show me which one he is. As you walk past him you're going to cough.

And she did, and when he left the café I followed him and saw him get into his Mercedes. I watched him drive away and I thought: Maybe. Maybe. Incha'Allah!

Once he had identified the man through his license-plate, he began to ask questions, first going to the qahouaji there in the café, and then having narrowed his search, to several merchants and bazaar-keepers in the city.

I found out more about him than his mother knows, said Bouselham. He owns half the textile factory at the Plaza Mozart, and an apartment house in the Boulevard de Paris. And three bazaars. So one night when I got home I took my sister up on the roof where we could talk, and I said to her: You like this Qasri?

She began to stammer and protest. I don't even know him. How can I say if I like him?

That made me angry and I grabbed her. You don't know whether you like him. But you got into his car and sat beside him. What does that mean?

She thought I was going to hit her, and she hid her face in her hands and backed away. I had the right to beat her, of course. But I let her know I was on her side, and would never mention it to the rest of the family. I even bought her new clothes the next day, so El Qasri could get some idea of how she could look if she wanted to. And I decided to wait and see if things happened by themselves.

He kept after her and she went on putting him off. Then once my father and mother and the whole family had to go to Meknes overnight, and she and I were the only ones who stayed home. I thought:

I'm going to spend the night in Tetuan and see what happens. So I told her I wasn't going to be there that night, and that she would have to sleep at our aunt's house. And I asked her please not to mention my trip to Tetuan to our parents, because of course I was supposed to be in the house taking care of her. I thought: If anything's going to happen by itself, tonight's the night when it'll happen. And I was right. I went to Tetuan and she went with him to his house, and it wasn't a long time later when she came to me and said she thought there was a child in her belly.

Right away I took her over to Gibraltar, to the biggest hospital. We stayed there four days, and I got the papers on each test, and there was no doubt about it, they said: there was a child inside.

Having nothing more urgent to do with his time, Bouselham continued to go each day to the café at the end of the city. Here he fell into conversation and eventual companionship with the rich merchant. Even after he had brought his sister back from Gibraltar, and the lawyer was busy preparing his strategy, even after the lawyer had called on the rich merchant to advise him that the only way of avoiding a scandal was to ask for the girl in marriage, before her family discovered her pregnancy, Bouselham sat daily with him in the café listening to the story of his troubled romance.

She's got a brother, the rich merchant told him. He's the one who wants my blood. The son of a whore found out about it.

Then Bouselham said to him: But why son of a whore? He's letting you marry her. If he wanted to, he could put you in jail today. Are you crazy? She was a virgin.

The rich merchant agreed that this was so. Less than a week later he made the offer of marriage to Bouselham's father.

After he stopped talking, I looked down at him, trying to see the expression on his face, but his head was outlined against the flames, and there was only the light of two candles in the room.

He's not going to like it much when he finds out you're her brother, I said.

He only laughed. Some day, he said. Some day.

I brought a fresh log, and he finally stood up.

Bouselham did not keep silent about the dubious part he'd played in the arranging of his sister's wedding; on the contrary, he discussed it at length with his Moroccan friends. To him it was a business matter in whose success he took a healthy pride. Thus several garbled versions of the story began to travel around Tangier. Mother heard them, but discounted them as fables invented purely out of spite. It was not until months after Bouselham's visit to me at the flat that she brought herself to accepting them as fact. At that instant she became irrational.

The whole thing is vile! she said. I've got rid of him. His dismissal had been summary, with no explanation offered. She had handed him a sum of money and told him to leave the premises instantly. Two days later she had set out for Italy. It was clear to me that she half expected to be blackmailed, but was ashamed to put it into words. If only she had mentioned her fear, I could have tried to reassure her. I believe I know Bouselham better than she did.

Until the day when he called to me from inside the Café Raqassa, I had not seen him for several weeks. We sat in a back corner where it was dark and the air smelled of damp cement and charcoal smoke. Bouselham spoke briefly of Mother, shaking his head ruefully. There was no mention of anything more than that he had lost his job as gardener when Madame went away. He was aware of somehow having offended her, but her arbitrary behavior had bewildered and aggrieved him. The way he saw it, he had been turned out of the house for no reason at all. Still, as we parted, he said: When you write to Madame, tell her Bouselham sends his greetings.

I did not pass on the message, or any subsequent ones, from him to Mother. She sold the house without returning to Tangier, and it seemed to me that living over there in Italy with Father she must be miserable enough without getting reminders of Bouselham from me.

Things Gone
and Things Still Here

Tangier—if I were to move into the house at Ain Chqaf I should go to great expense to have the workmen install a fountain in the center of the courtyard. The water would fall into a marble basin and run out along marble troughs into a ditch. Running water, they say, rests the soul before the hour of prayer. On occasion, perhaps too much. An example: the familiar story of Hadj Allal, who came to grief through no fault of his own.

"As if he had stepped on a mine," explained one divinity student. "Only the mine was invisible and made no sound when it exploded. No one knew anything about it. He was there looking into the stream. Then he came into the mosque. For all of us he had been out there perhaps five minutes. But in the place where he had fallen two years had gone by. He tried to explain it to us. We took him home and told his wife to put him to bed and cover him up."

There is the tale of the fqih who taught in a local mosque some two centuries ago. No trace of his passage through life would remain now had it not been for an inexplicable psychic misadventure: the man must have stumbled upon one of those rare fissures in time—an open fault, as it were, in the surface of time—and fallen in.

Another fqih, this one in Hajra den Nahal, is said to have slipped between two instants and fallen into a deep well of time. The accident occurred while he was washing in the stream outside the mosque. As he squatted by the running water two tolba passed by on their way into the mosque to pray. They were having a conversation. Later the fqih stated that he had heard only one phrase: "in the twinkling of an eye." That seems to have been the signal. Everything around him stopped existing and he was in darkness.

In all versions the entry into this bubble in time is decisive for the protagonist. The two false years, according to the Nahali's story, were spent by him in India in a state of invisibility. During that time he did nothing but observe a famous goldsmith at work. When he was cast out of the time trap and returned to the stream by the mosque, he had brought with him all the Indian master's secrets, knowledge which he immediately put to use by becoming a goldsmith himself. His fame as a master artisan spread throughout Islam, so that the Indian goldsmith, on hearing of it, could not rest until he had visited Morocco and seen the designs himself. Unwisely, he traveled with his wife. The dénouement and meaning of the story for those who tell it is the Nahali's double victory. Not only did the Indian see all his own designs improved upon by the Moroccan, but he also lost his wife to him.

Another unfortunate fqih passed his sojourn in the time bubble as a woman, but returned to the world with greater wisdom.

A brilliant account could be written of the saga of the Haddaoua and their destruction. The patron saint sat smoking kif in a nargilah all day every day, it is said; even seven or eight years ago adepts could still be found smoking beside the ruined tomb. The brotherhood has been painstakingly eradicated by the authorities. Sometimes you see a lone man walking along the road wearing the dusty rags and wild hairdo of a Haddaoui, but since the cult no longer exists (and, perhaps more importantly, has no headquarters) such a man no longer deserves the respect which being a member of a brotherhood would give him, and so for most citizens he slips into the category of ordinary madman.

In the eyes of the government, the Haddaoua were not a religious sect at all, but an organized group of brigands to be finished off with bullets. Apart from their uncanny powers over goats, which made it possible for them to arrange the wholesale theft of these animals all over northern Morocco, and their use of magic spells as a threat in order to extort money from the rural populace, there would seem to be no valid reason for their persecution and extermination. Perhaps it was the fact that they built a fortress and kept a good many women shut into the cellars. They claimed that the women had come of their own volition and asked to be taken in as adepts. Whether or not that was the case, once the women had been present at the rituals they were not permitted to leave the premises, but were locked into the basement where they performed domestic duties.

 The Haddaoua placed great stress on food. Each meal was a banquet. This emphasis on eating may have been a result of the vast quantities of cannabis the men ingested each day, but the meals themselves were made possible by the easy availability of edible livestock. A Haddaoui could go out alone into the countryside and return in a few days with hundreds of goats following him in single-file formation. This alone was enough to strike fear to the hearts of the peasants. No one appears to know exactly how they imposed their will on the animals, but all agree that it was a special art which took time and patience to learn. When you consider that the men learned the technique by lying down among the animals and conversing with them at night during their sleep, it does not seem so improbable. The Haddaoui lying in the Marrakech dust forty years ago "became" a goat while I watched, and there in front of me was a man's body with a goat inside it, as if the goat had been able to assume the visible form of a man, while at the same time it remained unmistakably a goat. Whatever it was that they stumbled upon in the way of esoteric knowledge, their misuse of it was their undoing.

 For people living in the country today the djinn is an accepted, if dreaded, concomitant of daily life. The world of djenoun is too close for comfort. Among the Moroccans it is not a question of summoning them to aid you, but simply of avoiding them. Their habitat is only a few feet below ours, and is an exact duplication of the landscape aboveground. Each tree, rock and house has its identical counterpart beneath the earth's surface. The only difference is that there the sky is made of earth instead of air, and so it is totally dark. But since the lower world is a faithful reproduction of the upper world, it follows that the djenoun are perfectly equipped for life down there, and actually prefer it to our world. The trouble occurs when they emerge and take on human or animal form, for they are our traditional enemies, an alien tribe always on the lookout for an opportunity to infiltrate our ranks, and they do this merely by establishing contact with us.

Once a djinn has revealed himself to you your life changes. You can suspect his influence or presence whenever things have not gone as they should have, whenever there is a suspect or inexplicable element in a situation, whenever, in short, you are confronted with anything you don't understand. This is your warning; you begin to look for the djinn, and sooner or later you come across it and recognize it, no matter in what form you find it. What counts is your behavior and method of dealing with it at that point. Losing out in your struggle with a djinn can involve you in years of harassment or illness; it can also be fatal.

Above all you must guard against becoming emotionally involved with a djinn or a djinniya. There are many instances of miscegenation, but these are usually not discovered until after one partner has killed the other. "I watched her for months and I noticed that she never ate anything with salt in it. That was how I knew she was not a woman."

The open points along the frontier between the two worlds can conceivably occur anywhere, but exist generally in caves and under water, particularly under running water. If your itinerary involves crossing a stream, best have something made of steel (or at least iron) handy. City people often say there are no djenoun, not any more, or in any case not in the city. In the country, where life is the same as before and where there are not many automobiles and other things containing iron, they admit that djenoun probably still exist. But they add that the automobiles will eventually drive them all away, for they can't stand the proximity of iron and steel. Then it will be only in the distant mountains and the desert where you will need to worry about them.

Notwithstanding the rationalizations, djenoun continue to raise havoc now and then in the very center of the city by coming suddenly out of sink drains and attacking housewives. With this in mind, many women will not allow any hot water to fall into the sink, which means they must wash the dishes in cold water for fear of burning the possible inhabitant of the pipe. Djenoun have been known to be extremely vindictive in such cases, and commonly retaliate by causing paralysis in the offender.

If you go to the outskirts of any town, to where the fields begin and sheep are grazing, and dig in the earth under certain trees, you will come upon a knife. If you dig somewhere a few yards away from there, you may find another. There are many of them, all of the folding sort, and each one is clasped shut on a scrap of paper. Even though you open every knife you find, each time releasing a man from the spell of some accursed woman, still you are not going to spend all your time doing good turns for a whole group of men you have never known and never will meet. There would be no reason in the first place to go and dig for knives unless you suspect that a woman has shut a knife on you. Then, depending on who you think it might have been and where she would be most likely to go in order to bury it, you get busy and start to dig.

Sometimes you come upon other men digging, and when they see you they look ashamed and pretend to be looking for some change they have dropped. Often they stand up, shrug, and walk away. But if you go some distance and wait, they come back and start again to dig. Where is the justice in a world in which a woman with a simple folding knife can make so much trouble for a man?

"Twice I've found folded knives deep in the water at the bottom of the cliffs along the strait. The women who do this are even worse than the ones who bury them in the ground. They are willing to walk all the way to the cliffs so they can ruin the lives of the men they hate. There is not much chance of these knives being found and opened. And even if the paper where the curse was written has dissolved in the water, the man can have no sort of life again until the blade is opened. It's the shutting of the blade on the curse that keeps a man from being able to get hard. If I ever come across a woman burying a knife, she'll never get back home."

Printed July 1977 in Santa Barbara for the Black Sparrow Press by Mackintosh and Young. Design by Barbara Martin. This edition is published in paper wrappers; there are 500 hardcover trade copies; 250 hardcover copies numbered & signed by the author; & 26 copies handbound in boards by Earle Gray lettered & signed by the author.

Photo: Angus Stewart

Paul Bowles has lived for many years as an expatriate American in Tangier, Morocco. He is the author of four highly acclaimed novels: *The Sheltering Sky, Let It Come Down, The Spider's House,* and *Up Above the World*. He has also written several volumes of short stories, including *The Delicate Prey* and *The Time of Friendship,* and in 1972 Black Sparrow Press published his Selected Poems, *The Thicket of Spring*. In 1965 Bowles met the young Moroccan, Mohammed Mrabet, with whom he has since collaborated on several novels and books of stories, the most recent of which, *The Big Mirror,* has just been published by Black Sparrow. Paul Bowles is also well known as a composer and is responsible for a collection of native North African music gathered for the Library of Congress.

Unless Recalled Earlier
Date Due

SEP 18 1987			
APR 18 1988			
APR 28 1988			
MAY 25 1988			
FEB 10 1991			
2/4/02			

BRODART, INC.   Cat. No. 23 233   Printed in U.S.A.